Tales of
Wisdom & Wonder

For Rowan, Alice and Liz, my most loyal — and critical — audience — H. L.
For Dermot — N. S.

Barefoot Books
2067 Massachusetts Ave
Cambridge, MA 02140

Graphic design by Jennie Hoare
Typeset in Meridien Roman 13pt
Color reproduction by Grafiscan, Italy
Printed and bound in China by Printplus Ltd

This book has been printed on 100% acid-free paper
Paperback ISBN 1-905236-84-0

3 5 7 9 8 6 4

The Library of Congress has cataloged the paperback edition as follows:

Lupton, Hugh.
 Tales of wisdom and wonder / retold by Hugh Lupton ; illustrated by Niamh Sharkey.
— Pbk. ed.
 v. cm.
 Contents: Monkey and papa god, Haitian — The curing fox, Cree — The peddler
of Swaffham, English — The white rat, French — The blind man and the hunter,
West African — Fish in the forest, Russian — The shepherd's dream, Irish.
 ISBN 1-84148-231-5 (alk. paper)
 1. Tales. [1. Folklore.] I. Sharkey, Niamh, ill. II. Title.

PZ8.1.L9738Tal 2005
398.2--dc22

2005000162

TALES OF
WISDOM
&
WONDER

RETOLD BY
HUGH LUPTON

ILLUSTRATED BY
NIAMH SHARKEY

Barefoot Books
Celebrating Art and Story

Contents

Monkey and Papa God
Haitian

Once upon a time, in the middle of a forest, there lived an old woman who kept bees. Hives and hives of bees she kept, and by the end of the summer she had honey: ladles, jars, bowls and barrels full to the brim with sweet, sticky, golden honey.

What was she going to do with it all?

Well, most of it she kept, some she gave away, and the rest she poured into a great pot. She lifted the pot up on to her head and set off through the forest towards the marketplace to sell her honey. Through the forest and through the forest she went, the great pot, brimful with honey, balanced on her head. But as she was walking a terrible thing happened.

She caught her foot on the root of a tree, she tripped, she fell and … SMASH! The pot was shattered and the honey was oozing and trickling this way and that way. The woman began to cry:

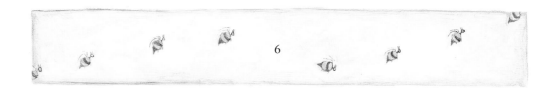

"Misery, oh misery, Papa God! Why d'you send me so much misery?"

And she made her way homewards, crying and wringing her hands:

"Misery, oh misery! Papa God, you send me too much misery!"

Now, sitting up among the branches of a tree, watching everything, was a little monkey. As soon as the woman was gone, the monkey swung down to the ground and dipped one of his fingers into this strange sticky stuff – he'd never seen anything like it before. He lifted his finger to his lips:

"Mmmmmm, this misery tastes good! I've never tried misery before." He scooped up a handful and swallowed it.

"Mmmmmm, misery is sweet, misery is sticky!"

He ate and he ate, gulping down the misery, spitting out the bits of stick and bark and licking the broken pieces of pot.

"Mmmmmm, misery is delicious!"

And when every last golden drop of it was finished, he had only one thought in his mind:

"I want more misery."

And then he remembered what the old woman had said –

"Papa God, why d'you send me so much misery?"– and he scratched his head. So that was where misery came from!

"Maybe," he thought to himself, "maybe if I paid a visit to Papa God, he'd give me some more misery."

The more he thought about it, the better the idea seemed to be.

So he climbed and he climbed and he climbed until he came to Papa God's house.

And there was Papa God himself, sitting in the sunshine, watching the world.

"Hey, Papa God!"

Papa God smiled.

"Ah, little monkey, what do you want?"

"Hey, Papa God, I want misery."

Papa God looked puzzled.

"You want misery, little monkey?"

"Misery is sweet, misery is sticky; I want as much misery as you can give me, Papa God!"

Papa God got to his feet.

"Well, it just so happens that I have got some special misery made for monkeys – if you're sure that's what you want?"

The monkey nodded his head. So Papa God went into his house. He was gone for a little while, and when he came out again he was carrying a leather bag.

"Little monkey, this bag is full of misery. Now, listen to me and do exactly what I tell you. First of all you must carry the bag to the middle of a great sandy desert, where no trees grow at all. Then you must open the neck of it, and inside you'll find all the misery you could ever dream of."

The little monkey didn't waste any time. He took the leather bag and he climbed back down to the world. He ran and he ran until he came to the edge of a great desert; he ran and he ran until he came to the middle of it. And then he sat down.

His belly was rumbling and his mouth was watering at the thought of all that misery.

He sat down and licked his lips and pulled open the drawstrings of the neck of the bag, just as Papa God had told him, and out came real monkey misery … DOGS!

One, two, three, four, five, six, seven huge, black, snarling, slavering dogs!

"Aaaaaargh!" The little monkey dropped the bag, turned on all fours and ran!

"Aaaaaargh!" The seven black dogs were after him!

"Aaaaaargh!" They were getting closer!

"Aaaaaargh!" He could feel their breath at his back!

And then, just when he thought his end had come … a tree appeared!

A great tree appeared out of nowhere. A great tree in the middle of the desert, where no trees grow at all. As fast as he could, the little monkey scrambled up among the branches.

And the seven dogs circled round and round the tree, growling and snarling and slavering – but dogs can't climb trees!

And all the rest of that day, the little monkey sat high among the branches of the tree, shaking and quaking with fear.

And when, at last, the sun set and the darkness came, the seven dogs went slinking away across the desert with their tails between their legs.

As soon as they were gone, the little monkey climbed down and ran back to the forest as fast as his legs could carry him.

But the question is this: who put that great tree in the middle of the hot, sandy desert where no trees grow at all?

I'll tell you: Papa God put it there. Why? Because Papa God knows that too much misery is not a good thing, even for a monkey.

The Curing Fox
Cree

Once upon a time there lived a young girl, and one bitterly cold day she fell ill. She fell ill with a terrible cough and a rattling pain in her chest so that it hurt to talk and it hurt even to breathe.

Her mother and father kept her warm with blankets and animal skins, but she didn't get better; she got steadily worse.

The light went out of her eyes and the life seemed to be leaving her. So her father and mother sent for the old healing woman, whose name was Duck Egg. Old, old, old she was – nobody knew how old – her face creased and folded and lined with wrinkles.

When old Duck Egg arrived, she hobbled across to the place where the girl was lying by the fire. Gently the old woman folded back the blankets and then leaned forward, pressed her ear to the pale skin of the girl's chest, and listened.

For a long time she listened, and the only sound in the room was the sound of the fast, painful breathing of the girl. For a very long time she listened. Then she lifted her head and spoke:

"The sound I hear is the sound of a she-fox. That fox is tired, running over the crusty hard snow. She is limping and her breath is raspy-hard. She is panting. Ohhhh, poor fox – she has a long journey to make. She is hungry. Every few steps she breaks through the snow crust … chhha – that's the sound I hear in the girl's chest."

And then the girl's father came across to the old woman and he said:

"Old Duck Egg, listen. I am a hunter. I will go out across the snow. I will catch the fox and bring her back to you."

And the old woman nodded her head and said:

"Yes, bring me the fox, bring the little she-fox to the village."

So the girl's father strapped on his snow shoes and set off, out of the village and away across the glaring white snow.

It was cold, bitterly cold. But there were tracks in the snow – fox tracks, footprints. Here was the place where the fox's tail had swept against the snow, and here the fox's feet had broken through the snow crust.

All day the girl's father followed the fox tracks, and just before darkness came he saw the fox. Thin and tired she was, running ahead of him through the snow.

Back in the village, old Duck Egg was listening carefully to the girl's chest:

"The sound I hear is the sound of a she-fox, but the hunter is close now – I can hear his snow shoes. He has seen her. Yes, he has seen the poor fox."

The girl's father kept on walking until it was too dark to see. Then he stopped and made a fire. He crouched beside the fire for warmth and he could see the fox's eyes gleaming in the darkness. She had stopped running; she was watching him.

Back in the village, old Duck Egg was listening carefully to the girl's chest:

"The sound I hear is the crackling of flames. The hunter has made a fire, the fox is watching. The girl will be very hot tonight. She will have a fever."

All night long the girl's father sat by the fire; he was cold and tired, but he did not fall asleep. When morning came, he set off after the fox again. Poor fox; she was very tired now, sick and weak she was, her feet kept breaking through the snow crust – chhha … chhha … chhha.

Back in the village the girl was coughing and coughing:

"Chhha … chhha … chhha."

And now the girl's father had caught up with the fox. He grabbed her in his hands. The fox was very frightened:

"Why have you followed me? Why have you caught me? I'm sick and tired. Kill me now. I can't run any more."

The girl's father could feel how thin the fox was. He could feel her bones and her heart beating.

"No," he said gently, "I will not kill you, little she-fox. I need you to stop a girl's illness."

And the girl's father turned with the little she-fox in his arms and made his way homewards across the snow.

Back in the village, old Duck Egg was listening carefully to the girl's chest:

"Her heart is beating very fast; the fox is frightened, the hunter is holding her tight in his hands. He is coming home now."

A day and a night it took the girl's father to make the journey homewards. When he reached the village it was morning. He came straight to where the girl was lying beside the fire.

Old Duck Egg was sitting beside her, and so was the girl's mother. When Duck Egg saw the hunter, she smiled so that the lines and wrinkles spread out from the corners of her eyes.

"Give me the fox. Give the little she-fox to me."

He gave the fox to the old woman – a limp bundle of fur in her hands. She made a place for the fox to lie in the warm firelight, on the soft furs and blankets of the girl's bed.

"Go and get her some food, fetch some meat for the little she-fox."

So the girl's mother fetched some meat and the fox ate; she ate and ate until all the meat was gone.

Then she slept for a long time. The girl slept as well. Both of them slept.

Old Duck Egg was very quiet.

The girl and the fox opened their eyes at the same moment.

The old woman said:

"Go and get some more meat!"

Again the fox ate everything.

"Now," said Duck Egg, "open the door flap and let the fox go."

The girl's father lifted the door flap. Old Duck Egg helped the girl to sit up.

The girl leaned against the old woman's arm and watched the little she-fox.

She watched the little fox sniff the air and run through the door. She watched her run away from the village and out across the snow, and as the sound of her footsteps grew fainter, so did the girl's coughing.

The fox's strength was back. She was running and running across the snow.

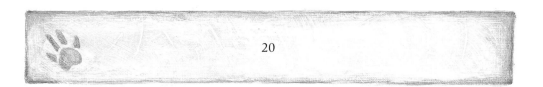

The girl got to her feet and walked to the door.

Her illness had gone. The fox had disappeared.

Old Duck Egg was quiet for a while, then she looked at the girl's father and mother.

"Answer this question," she said. "Did the fox cure the girl, or the girl cure the fox?"

The girl's mother put her hand on the old woman's shoulder:

"Neither. You cured both of them!"

And Duck Egg laughed then, and the lines and wrinkles spread out from the corners of her eyes.

The Peddler of Swaffham
English

Once upon a time there lived a man called John Chapman. He was a peddler by trade, and he tramped the streets, lanes and roads; he tramped the highways and the byways of England, selling pins and mirrors, ribbons and reels of thread, knives and scissors, pills and ointments and ballad sheets. And wherever he went, he would take his little dog with him, running at his heels.

Now, John Chapman and his dog lived in a little cottage on the edge of the town of Swaffham. A tiny cottage it was, and half open to the weather. In the spring the birds would be in and out of the broken windows, nesting in the rafters above his bed.

But he did have one little bit of luck. There was a tiny garden at the back of the cottage, and in that garden there was an apple tree, a beautiful old russet apple tree, and every autumn it would drop its fruit on to the grass – the sweetest apples in Swaffham.

22

Well, one night John Chapman was fast asleep in his bed when he heard a voice. He heard a lovely voice, as clear as moonlight, in amongst his dreams:

"Go to London Bridge," it said. "Go to London Bridge."

He woke up with a start, sat up, rubbed his eyes, looked about himself ... but the room was empty and dark, the only sound was the snoring of his little dog at the foot of the bed. "Nothing but a dream," he thought to himself, "nothing more than a dream."

And he rolled over and went back to sleep.

But the next night the voice was back, clear as moonlight in among his dreams:

"Go to London Bridge. Go to London Bridge."

He woke up; the room was dark.

"Nothing but a dream."

And he fell asleep.

But night after night the voice was back:

"Go to London Bridge."

And John Chapman started thinking to himself:

"Dreams are strange things and sometimes it's worth listening to them. Maybe I should listen to this one."

What would you have done?

Well, John Chapman thought about it and he thought about it, and in the end he said to himself:

"Yes! I've listened and I've heard and I'll go to London Bridge."

So he rolled his blanket into a bundle; he packed himself some bread and cheese; he whistled to his dog and he set off.

For two days he tramped and trudged along the highways and the byways, the roads, the lanes and the streets until at last he came to London Bridge, stretching over the River Thames.

In those days the bridge was all covered with shops, and there were people walking and people on horseback, there were carriages and carts moving this way and that way over it. He'd never seen such a hustle and bustle in his life.

What was he going to do?

What he did was this: he went to the top of the hump of the bridge and he stood and he waited … and nothing happened.

For a whole day he waited and nothing happened.

He spent a night sleeping on the embankment under the bridge … and nothing happened.

The next morning he went back up on to the bridge and sat on a doorstep … and still nothing happened.

He was hungry and he was cold and he started thinking to himself:

"Dreams are strange things. Sometimes it's worth listening to them … and sometimes it isn't."

And he was just getting up to his feet and thinking he'd start the long trudge home to Swaffham, when one of the shopkeepers opened the door of his shop, stepped down on to the pavement and looked at John Chapman.

"Now then, stranger," he said, "what's the matter with you? All yesterday I saw you standing over there on the hump of the bridge doing nothing, and here you've been all morning, sitting on a doorstep, shivering like a lost soul. What's going on, eh?"

And John Chapman said:

"Well, you see, I had a dream, and in my dream I heard a voice as clear as moonlight, and it said: 'Go to London Bridge.' And so I came …"

The shopkeeper threw back his head and bellowed with laughter:

"Dreams! Ha, ha, ha, ha! Stranger, listen to me: you don't want to take any notice of dreams! I'll tell you something. Last night I dreamed a ridiculous dream. I dreamed I was in a place called – what was it? – Swaffham … and there was a little cottage half

26

open to the weather … and I dreamed I was digging with a spade among the roots of an old russet apple tree … and there was a pot chock-full of gold … but do you think I'm going to cross half England in search of dream gold? Not me! Now, you listen to me and take my advice: if I was you I'd …"

But at that moment the shopkeeper saw that John Chapman was gone!

He was running through the streets of London with his dog at his heels! He didn't stop running by day or by night until he came home to Swaffham.

And he didn't waste any time there, either. He fetched a spade and he set to work, digging among the roots of the old russet apple tree. And sure enough, it wasn't long before the edge of his spade struck a large clay pot, which cracked open, and golden coins trickled down into the soil.

Hundreds of them! Thousands of them!

And from that moment John Chapman's peddling days were over; his tramping and trudging days were finished.

He had money enough to patch the holes in his roof and mend the glass of his windows.

He had money enough to eat whenever he was hungry.

And all the money that was more than enough (and there was plenty of it) he gave to the poor and the hungry and the homeless.

And so he lived happily to the end of his days.

And when he died, a statue was carved, a beautiful statue of John Chapman and his dog. It was set up in the marketplace in Swaffham, and carved into the stone at the foot of it were these words:

"Even dreams can turn to gold."

The White Rat
French

Once upon a time there lived a king and a queen who had no children of their own. The years passed and the years passed and still no children appeared, and so they adopted a white rat – a little, white, female rat with pink eyes and a long, twitching, whiskery nose … and how they doted on her!

All the talk in the palace was of her sweet nature, of her impeccable manners, her delicate little pink feet, her intelligence … and if anyone dared say a single word against her – it was the dungeons for him!

And so the time passed, with the white rat nibbling cheese from a golden bowl at the royal table, sitting on the golden arm of the king's throne when royal judgements were made, squatting between the ears of the queen's horse when she went riding across the kingdom.

Nothing in the world was as precious to that king and queen as their white rat.

And then, one day, a magician came to their palace, a magician, it was said, with tremendous powers.

As soon as the news of his arrival reached the ears of the king and queen, they sent for him.

"Magician," said the king, "do you have power enough to transform one thing into another?"

The magician bowed:

"Majesty, I do indeed."

"Do you have power enough to transform this charming creature," and the king picked up the white rat from the arm of his golden throne, "into a princess, into a human princess?"

And the magician bowed again:

"Majesty, I do indeed, but ..."

"But what?" said the queen.

"But although I have the power to change her outward appearance, I do not have the power to change her inmost, secret self."

And the king and the queen thought about her sweet nature, her manners, her delicacy, her intelligence, and they both said:

"We don't want you to change her inmost, secret self!"

So the magician bowed for the third time, then he raised his arms high above his head, shouted a strange word in a language the king and queen had never heard before, and struck his hands together.

There was a sudden blinding flash of light.

The king and queen covered their eyes with their hands.

And when they opened their fingers and lowered their hands, they saw that instead of the white rat there was a princess sitting on the golden arm of the king's throne.

And she was very beautiful – with just the faintest trace of pink in her beautiful eyes, and just the faintest twitch in the tip of her beautiful nose.

The king and queen were beside themselves with happiness.

They rewarded the magician with all the gold he could carry.

Then they ordered the finest dressmakers to set to work, cutting and stitching until the princess's wardrobe was full of magnificent clothes. They lavished her with all their attention, until they were sure that she wanted for nothing in the world.

And the years passed and the years passed.

And then, one day, the king decided that the time had come for the princess to get married.

"My sweetheart," he said, "it's time you chose yourself a husband."

And the princess smiled:

"Yes, Father, of course. But who do you want me to marry?"

"The choice is entirely yours. Just tell me who it is that your heart desires."

The princess thought for a moment.

"Then, Father, I would like to have as a husband the most powerful man in all the world."

Well, the king went away and thought about that. For three days he thought and thought, and then he called the princess before him.

"My sweetheart," he said, "I have decided that you should take the sun as a husband."

But the princess burst into tears.

"The sun! He's not powerful enough for me. It only takes one little cloud and all his light and heat are gone; all that's left is shivering shadow. No, I want a better husband than the sun!"

So the king went away and thought about that. For three days he thought and thought.

And then he said to the princess:

"My sweetheart, I have decided that you should take the cloud as a husband."

But again she burst into tears.

"The cloud! He's not powerful enough for me. It only takes one little puff of wind and he's sent scudding across the sky and torn to tatters. No, I want a better husband than the cloud!"

So the king went away and thought about that. For three days he thought and thought.

And then he said:

"My sweetheart, I have decided that you should take the wind as a husband."

"The wind! He's not powerful enough for me. It only takes one little mountain blocking his way and he has to turn aside. He might be able to bend the trees, but he can't shift a mountain for all his puffing and panting. No, I want a better husband than the wind!"

So the king went away and thought about that. For three days he thought and thought.

And then he said:

34

35

"My sweetheart, I have decided that you should take the mountain as a husband."

"The mountain! He's not powerful enough for me. It only takes one noble little rat with teeth like needles and claws like thorns to nibble and scrape a tunnel right into the heart of the mountain. Why, one brave little rat could make the mountain his palace. No, Father, I want a better husband than the mountain!"

So the king went away and thought about that.

For three days he thought and thought.

And then he said:

"My sweetheart, I have decided that you should take the rat as a husband."

And the princess threw her arms around the king's neck and kissed him on both cheeks.

"Yes, oh yes, the rat, the wonderful, handsome rat who can carve the mountain that blocks the wind that scatters the cloud that darkens the sun! The most powerful husband in all the wide world!"

And so it came about that the king and queen sent for the magician, and the magician stood before the princess:

he raised his arms, he shouted a word, he clapped his hands, there was a blinding flash of light … and a white rat crawled out from under the silken hem of the crumpled dress that had fallen in a sudden heap upon the floor.

And the magician bowed:

"I am sorry, your Majesties. As you may recall, I did not have power enough to change her inmost, secret self."

So the pretty little white rat was married to a handsome brown rat with teeth like needles and claws like thorns and a tail a yard long. And as for the king and queen, well, it wasn't long before they had hundreds of grandchildren – some brown, some white, some beige, some spotted … and how they doted on them all!

The Blind Man and the Hunter
West African

Once upon a time there was a blind man who lived with his sister in a hut in a village on the edge of the forest.

Now, this blind man was very clever. Even though his eyes saw nothing, he seemed to know more about the world than people whose eyes were as sharp as needles. He would sit outside his hut and talk to passersby. If they had problems, they would ask him what they should do, and he would always give good advice.

If there were things they wanted to know, he would tell them, and his answers were always the right ones.

People would shake their heads with amazement:

"Blind man, how is it that you are so wise?"

And the blind man would smile and say:

"Because I see with my ears."

Well, one time the blind man's sister fell in love; she fell in love

with a hunter from another village. And soon enough there was a wedding: the hunter was married to the blind man's sister.

And when the great wedding feast was finished, the hunter came to live in the hut with his new wife.

But the hunter had no time for his wife's brother, he had no time at all for the blind man.

"What use," he would say, "is a man with no eyes?"

And his wife would reply:

"But, Husband, he knows more about the world than people who can see."

The hunter would laugh then:

"Ha, ha, ha! What could a blind man know, who lives in darkness? Ha, ha, ha ..."

Every day the hunter would go into the forest with his traps and spears and arrows. And every evening, when the hunter returned to the village, the blind man would say:

"Please, tomorrow, let me come with you, hunting in the forest."

But the hunter would shake his head:

"What use is a man with no eyes?"

And the days and the weeks and the months passed, and every
evening the blind man asked:

"Please, tomorrow, let me come hunting."

And every evening the hunter shook his head.

But then, one evening, the hunter was in a good mood. He had
returned home with a fine catch, a fat gazelle. His wife had
prepared and cooked the meat, and when they'd finished eating,
the hunter turned to the blind man and said:

"Very well, tomorrow you will come hunting."

So the next morning they set off into the forest together, the
hunter with his traps, spears and arrows, leading the blind man
by the hand along the track between the trees. For hours and
hours they walked.

Then, suddenly, the blind man stopped; he tugged the
hunter's hand:

"Shhhh, there is a lion!"

The hunter looked about – he could see nothing at all.

"There is a lion," said the blind man, "but it's all right ... he's eaten and he's fast asleep. He won't hurt us."

They carried on along the track and there, sure enough, was a great lion stretched out fast asleep under a tree.

As soon as they had passed it, the hunter asked:

"How did you know about the lion?"

"Because I see with my ears."

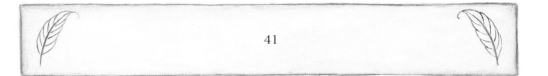

For hours they continued, and then the blind man tugged the hunter's hand again:

"Shhhh, there is an elephant!"

The hunter looked about – he could see nothing at all.

"There is an elephant, but it's all right ... he's in a water-hole. He won't hurt us."

They carried on along the track and there, sure enough, was a great bull elephant wallowing in a water hole, squirting mud on to his back.

As soon as they had passed it, the hunter asked:

"How did you know about the elephant?"

"Because I see with my ears."

And they continued deep, deep into the forest until they came to a clearing.

The hunter said:

"We'll leave our traps here."

The hunter set one of his traps, and he showed the blind man how to set another one. When both traps were ready, the hunter said:

"We'll come back tomorrow and see what we've caught."

And together they made their way home to the village.

The next morning they were up early. Once again they set off along the track into the forest. The hunter offered to hold the blind man's hand, but the blind man said:

"No, I know the way now."

The blind man walked ahead this time, and he didn't catch his foot on a root or a tree stump; he didn't miss a single turn.

They walked and they walked until they came to the clearing deep in the forest where the traps had been set.

The hunter saw straight away that there was a bird caught in each trap. And he saw straight away that the bird caught in his trap was a little grey one, and the bird caught in the blind man's trap was a beauty, with feathers of green, crimson and gold.

"Sit down there," he said. "We've each caught a bird. I'll fetch them out of the traps."

So the blind man sat down and the hunter went across to the traps, and as he went across he was thinking to himself:

"A man with no eyes will never know the difference."

And what did he do?

He gave the blind man the little grey bird, and he kept the beautiful bird with the green, crimson and gold feathers for himself.

And the blind man took the little grey bird in his hand and he got to his feet and they set off for home.

They walked and they walked, and as they were walking the hunter said:

"If you're so clever and you see with your ears, then answer me this: why is there so much anger and hatred and warfare in this world?"

And the blind man answered:

"Because the world is full of so many people like you – who take what is not theirs."

And suddenly the hunter was filled with bitter shame. He took the little grey bird out of the blind man's hand and gave him the beautiful green, crimson and gold one instead.

"I'm sorry," he said.

And they walked and they walked, and then the hunter said:

"If you're so clever and you see with your ears, then answer me this: why is there so much love and kindness and gentleness in this world?"

And the blind man answered:

"Because the world is full of so many people like you – who learn by their mistakes."

And they walked and they walked until they came home to the village.

And from that day onwards if the hunter heard anyone ask:

"Blind man, how is it that you are so wise?"

He would put his arm around the blind man's shoulders and say:

"Because he sees with his ears … and hears with his heart."

Fish in the Forest
Russian

Once upon a time there lived a farmer and his wife.

Now, the farmer's wife could not keep a secret! Can you keep a secret? The farmer's wife, she could not keep a secret.

Anything she was told, you could be sure the whole village would know about it before a day was over. And by the end of a week – what with her traveling to market, and visiting here and there, and delivering eggs to all and sundry – by the end of a week, you could be sure that everyone in the country would know about it. And if it was a thing worth knowing, you could be certain-sure it would have reached the ears of the king.

Nothing travels faster than gossip.

Well, one day the farmer was digging turnips in a field when suddenly the blade of his spade scraped against the iron lid of a rusty old chest.

And when he lifted the lid, his eyes were dazzled by a huge hoard of sparkling, yellow gold.

"Now, now," he thought to himself, "I must be careful. My wife can't keep a secret. If she sees this gold, the village will know about it in a day and by the end of a week the story will have reached the ears of the king. And him being a king, and a greedy one at that, he'll want all this gold for himself."

And the farmer sat in the field, and he thought and he thought. In the end he decided that the only thing to do was to wait for his wife to go to sleep, and then to bring the gold into the house in the middle of the night and bury it beneath the kitchen floor.

And that was what he did. He waited until she was fast asleep and snoring in her bed, and then, by the light of the moon, he crept out into the field and fetched the gold.

Carefully he carried it into the house and set to work, digging a hole in the kitchen floor.

But as he was digging, CRACK! The spade hit a rock.

His wife woke up. She lit a candle and came running down the stairs:

"What's going on down here?"

And then she saw the sparkling treasure!

"Oh, Husband, where did you find that gold?"

"Shhhh! Now listen, this gold is a secret. I found it in the turnip field. You mustn't tell anyone, not a living soul – do you understand?"

"Oh, Husband – you know me, I won't breathe a word of it to anyone. I promise!"

But could she keep a secret?

You know and I know and the farmer knew perfectly well that she could not keep a secret. All night long the farmer was thinking to himself:

"Now, now, what do I do next? Within a day the village will know, before a week's out it will have reached the ears of the king."

He thought and he thought and then he had an idea.

"Of course," he said, "that's what I shall do!"

And first thing in the morning, at the crack of dawn, he was out of bed and off to the village.

He went to the fishmonger's shop and bought some silver speckled trout.

He went to the baker's shop and bought some sweet currant buns.

And he went to the butcher's shop and bought a string of fat sausages.

Then he went into the forest, not far from his farm. He put the fish down on to the wet dewy grass, he set the buns along the branches of the trees, and he took a fishing line and hooked it on to the end of the string of sausages and threw them into the river.

Then, rubbing his hands together and chuckling to himself, he went back to the farmhouse:

"Wife, Wife, wake up! It's a perfect day for going fishing in the forest!"

His wife sat up in bed, rubbing her eyes:

"What? Fishing? In the forest?"

"That's what I said! Come with me quickly. It doesn't happen

often. There'll be fish swimming through the grass, and I'm told it's been raining cakes and buns!"

Well, she fairly leaped out of bed, flung on her clothes, grabbed a basket, and the two of them set off running across the fields to the forest.

They'd only just arrived when she shouted:

"Look here, look at this! It's true – here are trout swimming through the grass!"

She picked them up and dropped them into her basket.

"Lovely plump ones, too!"

Then she saw the buns along the branches:

"Husband! You were right. Buns!"

The farmer nodded:

"Aye, it's been raining cakes and buns all right. If you'd got out of bed quicker, I reckon we'd have found puddles of cakes on the ground as well. Someone got here before us and took them."

They hadn't gone much further when they came to the river. The farmer said:

"I'll just pull in my fishing line and see what I've caught."

He reeled in the line, and there, dangling at the end of it, was a string of fat sausages.

The farmer's wife gasped:

"Sausages! In the river!"

"Aye," said the farmer, "there are always sausages swimming in the river. Not everybody knows how to catch them, though."

And they went back to the farmhouse. And what a breakfast it was, with the plump trout, the sweet buns and the fat sausages.

But do you think the farmer's wife had forgotten about all that gold?

Of course she hadn't!

By the end of that day, the story of the hidden treasure had spread from one end of the village to the other. And by the time a week had passed (what with the farmer's wife traveling to market and delivering eggs to all and sundry), the story was known across the whole country.

After all, nothing travels faster than gossip.

And, sure enough, the story reached the ears of the king.

And, sure enough, being a greedy king, he wanted all the gold for himself.

"Bring me that farmer and his wife!" bellowed the king.

So the two of them were brought to the king's palace.

"Is it true," said the king, "that you have found a great hoard of treasure."

"No. It is not true. Not true at all," said the farmer.

"But your wife has been heard telling the story to all and sundry until the whole kingdom is talking about it."

And the farmer laughed.

"But, your Majesty, my wife is stark staring mad. She's as mad as a march hare. Her wits are quite addled!"

And his wife stamped her foot on the ground:

"I am not," she said."I saw him with my own eyes, your Majesty, hiding the gold beneath the kitchen floor."

And the king looked at the farmer's wife with his narrow, greedy eyes:

"When did you see this?"

And the farmer's wife thought for a moment, then she said:

"Well, your Majesty, it was the night before we found the fish swimming in the forest. It had been raining cakes and buns all night and we filled a basket ... and then my husband fished a string of fat sausages out of the stream ..."

And the king shook his head:

"Poor woman, quite mad, moonstruck, dizzy as a goose! Sausages in streams, fish in forests, gold beneath floors, raining cakes and buns! Take her home, farmer, and I shall never listen to her stories again."

And the two of them went home.

And so it was that the farmer kept all of that yellow, sparkling gold for himself.

And as for his wife, if she started telling secrets or spreading gossip, people would look at her and shake their heads and smile:

"She's moonstruck, poor thing!"

"Mad as a march hare!"

"Dizzy as a goose!"

So she started to keep her secrets to herself.

The Shepherd's Dream
Irish

Once upon a time there were two old shepherds. All day they'd been out with their sheep, and by the end of the day they were tired.

They set themselves down on some long soft grass beside a river. One of them stretched out, closed his eyes and soon he was fast asleep. The other sat, smoking his pipe, thinking about this and that, watching his sleeping friend.

It was a beautiful evening, the sun sending long shadows over the grass, the stream murmuring to itself …

Then, suddenly, a strange thing happened.

The sleeping man's mouth opened, and out of his mouth, between his lips, a white butterfly appeared.

A butterfly, as white as snow, was crawling out of his open mouth.

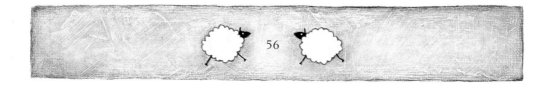

The butterfly crawled down the sleeping man's body, along one of his legs and then fluttered down on to the grass. There was a little path through the long grass to the stream, and the white butterfly made its way down to the water's edge.

The man who was awake got to his feet and followed this strange white butterfly – he'd never seen one like it before.

The path led to some stepping stones, and now the butterfly was fluttering from one stone to another until it reached the far side of the stream.

Stepping from stone to stone, the shepherd followed.

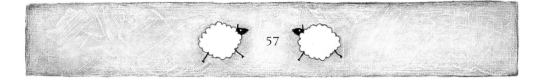

There were tall bulrushes growing on the far side, and now the butterfly was fluttering and flying in and out of them, weaving between them. The shepherd stood and watched, his pipe in his mouth, amazed. Then he saw, beyond the bulrushes, lying on the grass, there was a horse's skull. A great white horse's skull, weather-beaten and bleached by the sun.

58

The butterfly flew across to the skull. Then it fluttered over the clean white bone and flew in through one of the eye-sockets.

And the shepherd stood and watched as the butterfly searched and explored every corner of the skull.

After a while the butterfly came out again and flew back through the bulrushes, over the stepping stones and along the path. The shepherd turned quietly and followed it as it flew back to his companion and he watched in wonder as the butterfly crawled up the sleeping man's leg, over his body and into his open mouth. Straight away the sleeping man closed his mouth. Then he stretched and rubbed his eyes and awoke. He sat up in the grass and said:

"I must have been asleep for a long time."

"Not so very long," said his friend, "but while you were sleeping I saw a great wonder."

"You saw a great wonder! It is I who have seen wonders. Listen: while I was asleep I dreamed that I made a tremendous journey.

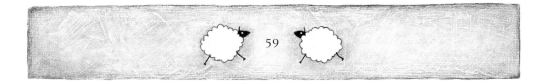

"First I traveled along a fine, wide road with great green hedges growing high on either side of me. At last I came to the edge of the sea. I set off over it, journeying from island to island until I reached a distant country. First I passed through a forest – such trees there were, I've never seen the like before, stretching high into the sky above my head. I was filled with wonder and delight and I wandered there for a while until I saw a palace. Oh, such a beautiful palace it was, built of shining white marble! I went in through the door and walked from one room to another. There was nobody to be seen – it was quite empty. I was just

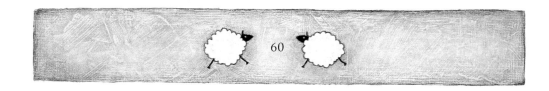

thinking that perhaps I would settle down and stay there for ever, when a strange feeling came over me and I knew I must go back the way I had come. So I left the palace and journeyed through the forest, over the sea, along the wide road, and at last I got home. I had just closed the door behind me and was thinking it was time to cook some supper when ... I woke up!"

His friend stood quietly for a while, puffing at his pipe, then he said:

"Come with me and I'll show you the journey you made."

And the man who had been sleeping got to his feet, and his friend told him about the strange white butterfly that had crawled out of his mouth.

"That little path," he said, "is the great wide road, and the grass growing on either side is the high green hedge. This stream is the sea and these stepping stones are the islands. Those bulrushes are the trees of the great forest and that horse's skull is the fine shining palace you went into – quite empty inside."

Both of them had seen wonders right enough!

But which of them had seen the greatest wonder?

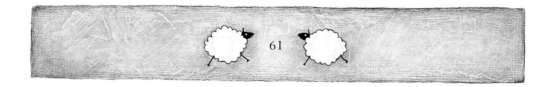

Sources

The storyteller's relationship with his sources is much the same as a jazz musician's relationship with melody. I have been telling many of these stories for years, so I make no apologies for the variations that have woven themselves around the tales as I received them. At the same time, I hope I've been true to the spirit of the tales, and to all those countless tellers who have carried them before me.

Monkey and Papa God

This story is widespread among the Caribbean islands and I've heard several variants of it, sometimes with "trouble" in the place of "misery." There is a version of it in Diane Wolkstein's wonderful collection of Haitian tales, *The Magic Orange Tree* (Schocken Books, New York, 1980).

The Curing Fox

There are many Native American tales about shamanistic healing journeys; this is one of my favorites. My source for this story is to be found in Howard Norman's extraordinary collection of Cree tales, *Where the Chill Came From* (North Point Press, San Francisco, 1982).

The Peddler of Swaffham

I've known this story since I was a boy; almost every storytelling tradition seems to have a variant of this theme. There is a version of it in Katherine Briggs's monumental *Dictionary of British Folk-Tales* (Routledge, London, 1991).

The White Rat

This is a French story that appears among the Auvergne folktales collected by Henri Pourrat. It is a variant of a story that crops up all over Europe and Asia. Indeed, there is an almost identical Indian tale called "The White Mouse." Henri Pourrat's version can be found in *French Folktales* (Pantheon Fairy Tale and Folklore Library, New York, 1989).

The Blind Man and the Hunter

I heard this story from my friend Duncan Williamson (Scotland's great bearer of traveler tales, ballads and lore), who in turn had heard it from a blind West African man in England. I have not found a printed version of this tale, nor do I know its exact country of origin. However, my favorite anthology of traditional African stories is Paul Radin's *African Folktales* (Schocken Books, New York, 1983).

Fish in the Forest

This is a Russian version of a motif that appears all over Europe. There is a fine Scottish variant called "Silly Jack and the Factor" which can be found in Katherine Briggs's *Dictionary of British Folk-Tales* (see above). My version came originally from an old anthology, *Folk Tales of All Nations*, edited by F. H. Lee (Harrap, London, 1931). Surprisingly, it does not appear in the definitive collection of traditional Russian stories, Aleksandr Afanasiev's *Russian Fairy Tales* (Pantheon Fairy Tale and Folklore Library, New York, 1973).

The Shepherd's Dream

This mysterious story appears in Sean O'Sullivan's *The Folklore of Ireland* (Batsford Books, London, 1974). It can also be found in Kevin Crossley Holland's *Folk-Tales of the British Isles* (Faber & Faber, London, 1985). Both are indispensable collections for anyone exploring traditional British tales.